WellieWishers™

Willa's Wilderness Campout

By Valerie Tripp

Illustrated by Thu Thai

★ American Girl®

Editorial Development: Jennifer Hirsch
Art Direction and Design: Jessica Rogers
Production: Jeannette Bailey, Caryl Boyer, Kristi Lively, and Cynthia Stiles
Vignettes on pages 82–85 by Flavia Conley

Parents, request a FREE catalog at **americangirl.com/catalog**.
Sign up at **americangirl.com/email**
to receive the latest news and exclusive offers.

For the Grandgirls,
with love

Meet the WellieWishers™

The WellieWishers are a group of fun-loving girls who each have the same big, bright wish: to be a good friend. They love to play in a large and leafy backyard garden cared for by Willa's Aunt Miranda.

Willa

Ashlyn

Emerson

When the WellieWishers step into their colorful garden boots, also known as wellingtons or *wellies*, they are ready for anything—stomping in mud puddles, putting on a show, and helping friendships grow. Like you, they're learning that being kind, creative, and caring isn't always easy, but it's the best way to make friendships bloom.

Camille

Kendall

GARDEN MAP

Carrot's Hutch

Chicken Coop

Playhouse

Garden Gate

Aunt Miranda's House

Garden Theater Stage

Greenhouse

Chapter 1

Campout Tonight!

Tonight's the night!" said Willa. "I can't *wait*. I'm so excited about our campout."

"Me, too!" cheered Camille, Kendall, and Emerson.

"Thanks for thinking up such a great new thing for us to do, Willa," said Kendall.

"I got the idea from this Wilderness Wendy book," said Willa, showing her book to her friends. "Wilderness Wendy says camping is really, really fun."

Emerson sang to the tune of "Yankee Doodle":

WellieWishers,
Shout hooray!
We'll surely have a ball!
Because tonight we're camping out,
The most fun fun of all.

"Wilderness Wendy says that the best part of camping is being outdoors, surrounded by nature," said Willa happily. "And I think so, too."

"Oh, I think the best part is putting up the tent," said Kendall, patting her tool belt. "It's like building a sweet little house."

"I think the best part is singing songs and telling stories and playing games," said Emerson. "And I *love* eating s'mores! They're *won*derful!"

"I think the best part is seeing the night sky full of magical, twinkling stars," said Camille dreamily.

Willa grinned. "It sounds like we're all ready to go camping right *now*."

"Where's Ashlyn?" asked Kendall. "I hope she didn't forget that tonight's the night."

Just then, Ashlyn staggered toward the girls.

"Holy cow, Ashlyn," said Willa. "What's all this stuff?"

"Kmpfinkg ekwpminnt," said Ashlyn.

"What?" giggled the girls. Emerson lifted a sleeping bag from Ashlyn's pile so that the girls could see and hear her.

13

"This is camping equipment," said Ashlyn. "I think I've thought of everything we'll need. Do you want to bring your teddy bear, Willa?"

"Bring my teddy bear on a camping trip?" scoffed Willa. "Of course not! Wilderness Wendy says you shouldn't bring anything that's not *strictly necessary*." She looked into one of Ashlyn's bags. "What's in this bag?"

"Bug repellent and mosquito netting," said Ashlyn. "They *are* strictly necessary, to keep away bugs and flies."

"Do you think there'll be *lots* of

bugs and flies?" asked Emerson, wrinkling her nose.

"I hope there *are*," gushed Camille, clasping her hands together. "Lots and lots of lightning bugs and fireflies. They're fairies in disguise."

Ashlyn smiled. "I wish fairies would help us get ready," she said. "But I'm afraid we're on our own. We have a lot to do before we go camping. Come on."

Is this enough bug repellent?

Bugs don't bug Wilderness Wendy!

The girls helped Ashlyn carry the camping equipment up the path to the playhouse.

I love putting up tents!

I can't wait for tonight!

Butterflies are fairies, too.

Ashlyn put down her armful of camping stuff, faced the girls, and said, "Now, the key to a successful camping trip is—"

"Getting away from civilization and living as simply and naturally as animals do," said Willa, reading aloud from her Wilderness Wendy book.

"Well, yes," said Ashlyn. "But also—"

"A cozy tent," said Kendall.

"A starry sky," said Camille.

"Fun and games and s'mores!" said Emerson. "And no bugs!"

"All those things are important," said Ashlyn, "but the key to a successful camping trip is *preparation*." She held up a roll of paper. "That's why I've made a list of the things that we need."

"A list?" asked Willa.

Ashlyn unrolled her list. It was long.

"In the wilderness you have to be prepared," said Ashlyn. "We'll need water, shelter, and food."

Willa shook her head. "Animals live in the wilderness, and *they* don't lug equipment with them," she said. "Wilderness Wendy says the whole *point* of camping is being simple and natural."

"I thought the whole point was having fun," said Emerson.

"If you want, I can organize this stuff and gather all the other supplies that we need," Ashlyn offered.

"*More* stuff?" asked Willa. "*Real* campers don't need—"

But Kendall spoke over her. "It wouldn't be fair for you to do all the work, Ashlyn," she said. "Would you like to divide up your list and give each of us part of it?"

"Okay," said Ashlyn. She carefully tore her list into five parts, added a few words to each one, and gave each girl part of the list.

"We'll meet at sundown at the camping spot," said Willa, "and then the fun can begin!"

As the girls left the playhouse, Ashlyn reminded them, "Don't forget to pack the stuff on your lists!"

"We won't!" said Camille, Emerson, and Willa, as Kendall scurried back to the playhouse to get her left-behind list.

Chapter 2

Ready for Fun

Kendall found her part of the list on the workbench, and she found her hammer, too. *We might need this,* she thought. As Kendall slipped her hammer into her tool belt, a gust of wind blew her list off the workbench, out the door, and up into the sky like a kite. "Hey, list!" shouted Kendall. "Where are you going?"

Kendall jumped as high as she could and tried to catch her list, but *snatch*! A bird swooped down and caught the list in its beak. "Yoo-hoo, bird," hooted Kendall. "May I please have my list back?"

Too-wheet! the bird answered
sweetly, but she did not return the list.
Instead, she used it as part of her nest.

Kendall grinned. "Okay, Mrs. Bird,"
she said. "You've found a good use for
my list, though it's not *egg*-zactly what
Ashlyn had in mind!"

As Camille skipped off with her list, she saw a shimmering dragonfly. Enchanted, Camille followed the dragonfly to the pond, which was surrounded by tall, shiny green grass. *This grass is pretty*, thought Camille. *I'll pick some so we can make friendship bracelets at our campout.*

While Camille was gathering the grass, she heard a frog croak, *Ribbit*. The frog sounded sad.

"Oh dear, you're stranded on that lily pad," Camille said. "I bet you're an enchanted prince, like in a fairy tale! I'll help you, my friend. Hang on." Camille flung her list onto the surface of the pond. "Here's a paper lily pad for you, Prince Ribbit."

Hop! The frog jumped onto the paper lily pad. *Hop!* From the paper lily pad, it jumped to the bank. *Ribbit, ribbit,* the grateful frog croaked as it hopped away.

"Good-bye, Prince Ribbit!" called
Camille. "I hope your fairy tale has a
hoppy ending!"

Using a long stick, Camille fished the paper lily pad out of the pond. *Uh-oh*, she thought. Her list was sopping wet. Camille shoved it into her pocket, thinking, *I'll read it when it dries*. She went back to gathering pond grass, humming happily.

Emerson gathered the things on her list. She packed a sleeping bag, a flashlight, a water bottle, and a bag of marshmallows. Then she picked up her dinosaur puppet and her rubber chicken. "Sorry," she said. "Since I packed all the camping stuff, there's no room in my pack for you two."

"Don't leave us behind," Emerson made her dinosaur puppet say. "We're *fun* stuff."

Pawk, pawk, pawk! she made her rubber chicken agree.

"Camping *is* supposed to be fun," Emerson said. She turned her pack upside down and dumped the

sleeping bag, flashlight, and water bottle in a pile on the floor. Then she put her dinosaur puppet and her rubber chicken in her pack and popped a marshmallow in her mouth, thinking happily, *Without all the boring camping stuff, there's plenty of room in my pack for the fun stuff!*

Willa sat on a log by Carrot's hutch. "Our campout isn't shaping up the way I imagined it," she said to Carrot. "Look at this list that Ashlyn made: tent, sleeping bag, flashlight." Willa shook her head. "Wilderness Wendy builds a shelter out of sticks and sleeps on a bed of leaves under the shining stars. *I* want to be a *real* camper, like *her*."

Willa folded her list into a paper hat. "I'll make my list useful," she said to Carrot. "I'll use it as a sun hat. That's exactly the sensible kind of thing that Wilderness Wendy would do."

The sun was just beginning to go down when the girls met at the camping spot.

"Wow, Ashlyn," said Willa. "You've already set up your tent?"

"Yes," said Ashlyn. "I came early so I could help the rest of you. We have just enough sunlight left to set up your sleeping bags and unpack the things from your lists."

The other girls looked at one another uncomfortably.

"You did bring sleeping bags and the other things on your lists, right?" asked Ashlyn.

"A mother bird snatched my list and used it as part of her nest before I read it," said Kendall.

Camille held up her list, which was a soggy mess. "My list got too blurry to read after Prince Ribbit used it as a lily pad."

"Here's my list," said Willa, pointing to her head. "I'm using it as a sun hat. That's what Wilderness Wendy would do."

"I sort of ignored my list," said Emerson, "except for the part about marshmallows."

"What *did* you all bring?" asked Ashlyn.

"I brought pond grass," said Camille. "We can use it to braid friendship bracelets."

"I brought my tools," said Kendall, "in case we need to build something."

"I brought my Wilderness Wendy book," said Willa, "so I can follow her advice and camp the way real campers do."

"I brought puppets to entertain you," said Emerson. She held up the dinosaur puppet and the rubber chicken and made them say, "Hi, WellieWishers! Thanks for including us. *Pawk, pawk.*"

Wilderness Wendy

"So let me get this straight," said Ashlyn. "*Not one* of you brought a sleeping bag or any of the other stuff on your list, except for Emerson, who brought marshmallows?"

Camille, Kendall, Willa, and Emerson shook their heads.

"Don't worry about us, Ashlyn," said Willa. "We'll be fine. Nature will provide everything we really need."

"We'll be *egg*-cellent," Emerson made her rubber chicken say.

"We're ready for the fun to begin!" said Camille. "Hooray!"

Chapter 3

N'more S'mores

Willa and Kendall went right to work gathering sticks and fallen branches for a shelter like the one in the Wilderness Wendy book. Camille began braiding friendship bracelets out of the pond grass. She gave the first bracelet to Ashlyn.

"Oh, this is really cute!" said Ashlyn

as Camille put the bracelet on her wrist. "Thank you!"

"You're welcome. I'm glad you like it," said Camille. "It's called a mermaid braid. See how the end fans out like a mermaid's tail?"

"Will you make me one?" asked Emerson. Then she made her dinosaur puppet and rubber chicken ask, "And me? And me?"

"Sure!" said Camille. "I'll dive right in! Three mermaid tails, coming up."

"Come see our shelter," Willa said to Ashlyn.

"Wow," said Ashlyn. "This is cool. I've never seen anything like this before."

"It's called a lean-to," said Willa. "We made it out of sticks and branches we found on the ground."

"We learned how to make it from Willa's Wilderness Wendy book," said Kendall.

"See, Ashlyn?" said Willa. "We don't need to worry about tents."

"You're right," said Ashlyn. "I guess I was silly to fuss." She smiled. "I have an idea—let's make s'mores!"

"Yes!" said Kendall.

"Now you're talking!" said Willa.

"I'm starving!" said Emerson.

"Me, too," said Camille.

"Kendall, you brought the graham crackers, right?" said Ashlyn.

"The what?" asked Kendall. "Crackers? Me?"

"They were on your list," said Ashlyn.

"Uh-oh," said Kendall.

"Camille, how about the chocolate?" Ashlyn asked.

"So *that's* what this says," said Camille, squinting at her waterlogged list. "I thought that word was *chompmate*, and I did *not* know what *that* was."

"Marshmallows were on my list and I *did* bring them," boasted Emerson, holding up the bag. Then she saw that the bag was empty. "Whoops! Sorry! I—um—I guess the dinosaur and chicken got hungry and ate all the marshmallows." She scolded her puppets. "Nice going, you two."

"So," said Ashlyn. "N'more s'mores. Oh well."

"That's okay," said Willa. "Wilderness Wendy would say that s'mores are *not* strictly necessary. In fact, none of the stuff on your lists is really necessary. Not for *real* campers, anyway."

Ashlyn's face turned pink. Then she took a deep breath and said quietly, "I guess Wilderness Wendy and I have different ideas about what's necessary for camping."

"She's the expert," said Willa, hugging her book.

"Well, I'm cold and hungry, so I'm going to head into my tent for a snack," said Ashlyn. "Does anyone want to join me?"

"No," said Willa, before anyone else could answer. "We'll be fine. Don't worry about us."

"Ohh-kay," said Ashlyn.

Camille turned to Willa. "Why'd you say we're fine?" she asked. "I'm so hungry I could eat a friendship bracelet!"

"I'm hungry, too, and cold," said Kendall. "I wish I had my sleeping bag."

"Are we going to have to sleep out here with all the bugs?" asked Emerson.

"Maybe we should have paid more attention to Ashlyn," said Camille miserably. "Everything we want now was on her lists."

"Come on, you guys," said Willa.

"Stop complaining! 'Fun' wasn't on any of Ashlyn's lists, but we can still have some, right?"

"Emerson to the rescue!" shouted Emerson, waving her puppets in the air. "I'll put on a puppet show."

"Oh, please, no," said Camille. "I'm so starving, that rubber chicken is starting to look delicious to me."

"Yikes!" said Emerson, hiding the rubber chicken behind her back.

"Okay, I'll admit it: Ashlyn was right about the lists," said Kendall. "Everything was easy-breezy until the sun went down. But now it's dark and cold and time for dinner."

"Yes," agreed Emerson. "I wish I had brought a sleeping bag instead of all this fun stuff." She spoke to her puppet and her rubber chicken. "Sorry, you two, but it's true."

"I should have read my list before I let Prince Ribbit use it as a lily pad," said Camille. She sighed. "What are we going to do?"

Chapter 4

What's Missing?

Kendall stood up. "I think we all know what we should do."

Camille nodded, "Tell Ashlyn we're sorry—"

"And ask her for *food*!" Emerson moaned. "I think Ashlyn has *cocoa*."

"Are you with us, Willa?" Kendall asked.

"No," said Willa. She sat on top of her Wilderness Wendy book and wrapped her arms around her legs. "I still think *real* campers shouldn't need so much fussy, fancy stuff."

"What will you do out here in the dark?" asked Kendall. "You'll be all by yourself."

"Except for the bugs," added Emerson.

"Oh, I'll be perfectly happy looking at the stars," said Willa. "Wilderness Wendy says that camping is about enjoying nature, and it has everything we need. So I want to be in the great outdoors, not inside a tent. Really, trust me, I'll be fine."

"All right," Camille said gently. "You do what you want, Willa. The rest of us will be in Ashlyn's tent."

"We *hope*," said Emerson.

"Knock, knock," said Camille, outside Ashlyn's tent. "Anybody home?"

Ashlyn poked her head out. "Hello!" she said. "Are you guys having fun?"

"NO!" wailed Camille, Emerson, and Kendall.

"Ashlyn, we should have listened to you," said Kendall.

"You tried to help us be prepared," said Emerson, "and boy, are we ever *not*."

"We didn't bring the right stuff," said Kendall.

"You gave us lists, and we didn't pay attention to them," added Camille. "Now it's cold and dark and we're hungry—"

"*And sorry!*" Kendall, Emerson, and Camille said together.

Ashlyn flung open the tent flap and welcomed her friends inside. "Don't worry; I brought extra of everything!" she said. "Come on in!"

"*Oooh,*" the others sighed when they stepped inside Ashlyn's tent and saw the sleeping bags and food. "Thank you, Ashlyn!"

"You're welcome," said Ashlyn. "It'll be a little crowded."

"That's okay!" said Camille. "It'll be warmer that way."

"We're *f-f-f-frozen*," said Emerson with a shiver.

"Have some cocoa," said Ashlyn. "It will defrost you." She began to pour the cocoa, and then she paused. "Wait. Where's Willa?"

"Willa's outside with the stars and the bugs," shuddered Emerson.

"Oh, dear," said Ashlyn. She peeked out at Willa. "I bet she's lonely out there."

"Willa wants to sleep outside and enjoy nature," said Kendall, "because Wilderness Wendy says that nature has everything we need."

"Well, *I* think that Ashlyn has everything we need in *here*," said Camille as the girls sipped their cocoa.

Ashlyn shook her head. "One important thing is missing," she said.

"I think I know what it is," said Emerson with a smile.

"Me, too," said Kendall.

"Me, three," said Camille. "And I know *where* it is, too. It's outside, right?"

"Come on," said Ashlyn. "Let's go."

Chapter 5

Strictly Necessary

Sitting alone in the lean-to, Willa shivered. It was awfully cold, dark, and lonely, even under the great big beautiful starry sky. *I wish I had my teddy bear to keep me company*, thought Willa, fighting back tears.

Just then, all the other girls stuck their heads out of the tent. "Hey, Willa," called Emerson, "you know how Wilderness Wendy says you should only bring what's strictly necessary on a campout?"

"Yes," said Willa.

"Well, it turns out we're missing something strictly necessary," said Ashlyn.

"What's that?" asked Willa.

"YOU!" said all her friends.

"Please, may we join you?" Camille asked. "We want to sleep out under the stars with you."

"I would love it if you did!" said
Willa happily.

Ashlyn gave Willa a sleeping bag, and the girls put their pillows in a circle with their heads together.

"Oh, look!" said Camille, enchanted. "The fireflies are dancing under the stars like fairies. Aren't they pretty?"

"Mmm-hmm," agreed all the girls softly.

Quietly, they watched the flickering fireflies swoop and swirl under the twinkling stars.

"I'm glad you're all out here with me," said Willa. She snuggled in her cozy sleeping bag and said to Ashlyn, "Thank you for bringing this extra sleeping bag. It's a good thing you were so well prepared."

"Well, I might have been a bit *too* prepared," Ashlyn said with a grin. "It turns out that we don't need a tent. You were right; it's even better sleeping under the stars, like Wilderness Wendy."

"If you ask me," said Emerson, "we were *all* wrong about the most important part of camping out. It isn't what you bring or what you do; it's the friends you're with." Softly, she sang a lullaby to the tune of "Yankee Doodle":

WellieWishers, close your eyes.
It's time to sleep and rest.
And dream of all the fun we'll have
Together—that's the best.

Willa smiled and said,
"Let's write to Wilderness
Wendy and tell her that there's
only one thing real campers need
for a really great camping trip:
good friends!"

"Yes," said Ashlyn, "friends
aren't on any list—"

"But," said Willa,
"they are definitely
strictly necessary."

Easy Backyard Camping

Camping is a great way for kids to learn about nature and to bring friends and family together. A campout doesn't have to be in a state or national park to provide a fun learning experience and great memories. It doesn't even have to be overnight! But as the WellieWishers learned, camping is more fun with friends. So help your girl round up a few siblings or friends, and have a campout without even leaving the backyard!

Pitch a Simple Tent

All you need is:

- 1 large sheet, light colored
- 1 old blanket or quilt
- 1 sturdy rope
- 12–16 rocks, bricks, or canned goods

Select two trees about 8–12 feet apart. Tie each end of the rope to a tree, and help your girl drape the

sheet over the rope. Lay the blanket or quilt on the ground, centered under the rope. Then gently stretch the sheet out over the blanket on each side to create a tent. Hold down the edges of the sheet with rocks, bricks, or cans. This tent won't be weatherproof or mosquito-proof, but it will offer a cozy hideaway for naps and overnight stays in good weather.

Even if the children won't be sleeping overnight in the tent, they will enjoy playing and resting in it. Invite them to spread out sleeping bags or blankets, pillows, and a few stuffed animals, books, coloring supplies, and games. But leave the electronic toys at home—a key part of camping is being unplugged!

Crunchy Munchies

Traditional camping fare includes trail mix, which is simply a mixture of any of these ingredients:

- Pretzels
- Small cheese crackers or bagel chips
- Raisins or other dried fruit
- Chocolate chips or small candies
- Peanuts, almonds, or other nuts
- Seeds, such as sunflower or pumpkin

You'll need about 1 cup of ingredients per camper. Before the campout, have your girl choose the ingredients, mix them together in a bowl, and then scoop the mix into small plastic bags, one for each camper. (If there are any food sensitivities in the group, prepare snack bags for those campers separately with appropriate ingredients, and label them.) Pass out water bottles or juice boxes, too.

Play I Spy

Even in a familiar setting, there are always new things to see. Take a "hike" around your yard, and when you spot something interesting, say "I spy with my little eye . . ." followed by a loose description of the item. For example, ". . . something that flies" (for a bird or butterfly), "something spiky in a tree" (for a pinecone), "something with yellow petals" (for a flower). Who can find the mystery item first? Then gather to look closely at it. Does anyone know what kind of bird, tree, or flower it is? What else is interesting about it? Take turns spotting items for the others to find.

Make a Leaf Rubbing

Capture the beauty of leaves with crayons. You will need:

- Folded newspaper or magazines
- White paper
- Crayons with the paper peeled off

Send the campers around the yard to collect a few pretty leaves, grasses, and ferns. (Flowers don't work well unless they're flat. If there are plants the campers shouldn't pick, let them know.) Set folded newspaper or a magazine on a flat surface, one for each camper. Have the children arrange their leaves on top and place a sheet of white paper over their leaves. Show them how to lay the crayon on the paper like a log, and rub it back and forth over the leaf, pressing firmly. The outlines and veins of the leaves will pick up more of the crayon color and show through the paper. The rubbings will make a unique and artistic keepsake of your campout to display at home.

Night Magic

There's something very special about being outside at night! Gather on a blanket in an open area, turn off all the lights, and listen. What do you hear? Are there nighttime bird or insect noises? Look up— can you see any stars? If a lot of stars are visible, keep watching to see if anyone spots a shooting star! (Late July and mid-August are especially good times to see shooting stars.) If you see three stars lined up in a row, point it out: That's the belt of the constellation Orion, the Hunter.

Send one or two children into the tent, and have them turn on a flashlight and point it at the side of the tent. (If they want, they can leave the flashlight in the tent and come back outside with the group.) Wait a few minutes to see if moths or other night-flying insects land on the tent. If they do, take a close look. Are their bodies smooth or fuzzy? How many legs do they have? Can you see their eyes or antennae?

Bedtime Fun

Just before bed, tell some stories (funny stories, not scary ones, for this age group) and sing a few favorite songs. If a parent or older sibling can play guitar, that will make the evening extra special. Then tuck the little ones into their sleeping bags—or their beds if they're not quite ready to spend the night outside. That can be something to save for a future camping adventure!

About the Author

VALERIE TRIPP says that she became
a writer because of the kind of person she is.
She says she's curious, and writing requires you
to be interested in everything. Talking is her
favorite sport, and writing is a way of talking
on paper. She's a daydreamer, which helps her
come up with her ideas. And she loves words.
She even loves the struggle to come up
with just the right words as she writes
and rewrites. Ms. Tripp lives in
Maryland with her husband.